the Magical I

The Power of Your Thoughts

MW00952979

"You are the author of your own story."

Created by Alexandra Angheluta
Illustrated by Polina Hrytskova

Vera loves to play in her room. No one knows exactly why, because it is quite empty. Vera doesn't have any toys.

But that doesn't matter.
She has the one thing that
she needs most,

her imagination.

Vera's laughter usually fills the house.

But lately, it has been quiet.

Vera has been feeling concerned

because she has noticed that her

parents have not been smiling as often.

Even though her room is full of joy, her house seems strange and dark. Vera overheard her parents talking in the kitchen last night.

They are worried that they don't have enough money to buy Vera toys for Christmas.

Vera tried to show her parents
that she doesn't need toys!
She has so much fun in her room:
there are mermaids, unicorns
and fairies to play with!
But every time her mom walks
in her room, all she could see
is a room with a bed.

Why do they all disappear when her parents walk in?
Vera doesn't understand! She knows they exist!
She has seen them! She has heard them!
She has played with them!
When alone in her room,
they go on so many
adventures together.

In the mornings, Vera always spends time with her pet: Bianca!

They ride through the forest to find beautiful flowers.
Vera uses the petals to paint her hair the colors of the rainbow.
This makes her feel as enchanted as a unicorn.

In the afternoons, she and Bianca must go and
save the fairies! The dragons keep capturing
them and locking them up:
they want their mystical fairy dust!

However, the dragons are no match for the power that comes out of Bianca's horn.

In the evenings, Vera always goes for a swim with her best friend: Coral.

Coral is a mermaid, so she knows
all the best hiding spots in the sea.
The evil sea serpent can't
ever find them!
Vera feels so safe
in this world.

One night, Vera tells her parents all
about her adventures.
They do not believe her;
they think she is pretending!
She is most certainly not!

Vera stood up and said:

"I believe in *magic*.
I believe in *miracles*.
I believe anything is *possible!*"

After these precious words were spoken, two fairies flew into the room and sprinkled fairy dust all over her parents! Vera couldn't help but giggle seeing her mom and dad so sparkly!

But what surprised Vera the most was when she heard both of her parents say:

"We *believe* in magic. We *believe* in miracles. We *believe* anything is possible!"

Vera felt so happy to hear her parents speak those powerful words.

She was full of hope!

Maybe her parents would join her on her adventures.

Maybe they would play with her.

Maybe her parents would finally see what she sees!

Maybe they would smile more.

Vera's mind was full of *possibilities*.

Vera was so excited that she couldn't sleep! Coral, Bianca and the Fairies stayed up with her all night. They were determined to come up with a plan that would help her parents see the magic around them.

They decided that the fairies would
sprinkle pixie dust on their foreheads.
A teaspoon just before they fell asleep,
and another right before waking up!

And the mermaids' lovely voices
would sing in their dreams:

"Miracles are natural. Magic is real.
You will see it once you believe it."

As the days passed, Vera noticed that her parents were smiling more. They had a light glowing around them that grew brighter with each day.

Though they still were not able to see the mystical creatures in her room, they started to have some wonderful moments playing together.

Together, they trained the dragon to be the protector of the castle. The Fairies lived freely and added so much beauty to their world.

They even went on underwater sea adventures!
Vera was overflowing with love. She felt so connected.

And then a miracle happened!

Vera's parents stepped into her room on Christmas morning and saw the magic. All she ever wanted was her parents to see this miraculous world. Her Christmas wish came true.

Her mom and dad embraced Vera. Their eyes sparkled with happiness. They said to her:

"You are the most magical creation,
you are proof that magic exists.
Thank you for helping us believe.
You are the best gift."

And from that Christmas on, Vera's family
lived in a world of unlimited possibilities.
They went on a journey and
saw that magic is always around.
It is just visible to those who believe in it.

Dear parents,

My hope is to help create a generation of children who find that everything they need, is truly within them. It all starts with our thoughts, beliefs, and the words we say. Once we change our inner dialogue, our external lives change as well.

By teaching children to use positive words, they become more confident, peaceful and compassionate children. Let's help them foster authentic self-love, which can lead to more loving and positive relationships.

I recommend practicing the affirmations on the following page daily! Affirming these words while in a yoga pose is even more beneficial, as children experience the power of positive words while connecting to their bodies for an integrated experience.
Sit in lotus pose while affirming: "I am peaceful".
Stand tall in tree pose while affirming: "I am strong".
Move into warrior pose while affirming: "I am brave".
Not only will your child help water the belief of unlimited possibilities within themselves, they will learn to be present and mindful.

I wish you and your child the best on this journey of personal transformation and deep connection!

Affirmations for Positive Thoughts

I am creative.

I inspire those around me.

I am radiant, beautiful and strong. I love who I am.

I have loving relationships with the people in my life.

I am kind and compassionate.

I appreciate everything I have.

I am a powerful creator. I embrace life with passion and joy.

I am enough. I do enough. I have enough.

I express my feelings. I am loved.

I am in control of my thoughts. I choose to be positive.

I take care of my body and mind.

Everything will be okay.

About the Author

Alexandra was born in Romania. When she was 4, her parents immigrated to America in hopes for a more safe, secure and abundant life for their family. She now spends her time in Portland, Oregon playing with children, writing in nature and connecting to spirit on the yoga mat.

Alexandra has been connecting with children through imaginative play for more than a decade. With an educational background in social work and play therapy, she was inspired to create stories and art for children.

Alexandra is the creator of the Magical Affirmations series. All of the books focus on healing from within by using positive thoughts and words. The books focus on emotional growth topics such as self-love, grounding/safety, faith, courage, positive thinking, connection, using your voice, and inner light.
She is a believer that play and words of affirmation have the ability to transform.

Magical Affirmations

Thank you for your purchase! If you enjoyed this book, please leave a review on Amazon. Reviews help these books get into little hands to help spread more light and love!

The following Magical Affirmations books are now available:

- The Magical Globes: The Power of Having Faith

- The Magical Gray Flower: The Power of Self-Love

- The Magical Dreamcatcher: The Power of Believing in Your Inner Light

- The Magical Mind: The Power of Your Thoughts

You can follow Alexandra @magical_affirmations and @alexandra_angheluta to stay updated on new releases.

To My Parents

This book is dedicated to my parents.
Thank you for believing in your dream and having
the courage to follow through to create a better
life for our family.

Copyright © 2020 by Alexandra Angheluta

All rights reserved. This book or any portion thereof may not be reproduced or used in any manner whatsoever without the express written permission of the publisher except for the use of brief quotations in a book review.

Created in Portland, Oregon. United States of America
First Printing, 2020
Library of Congress Control Number: 2020903015
ISBN: 9798613638277

Made in United States
Troutdale, OR
12/05/2024

25948887R00021